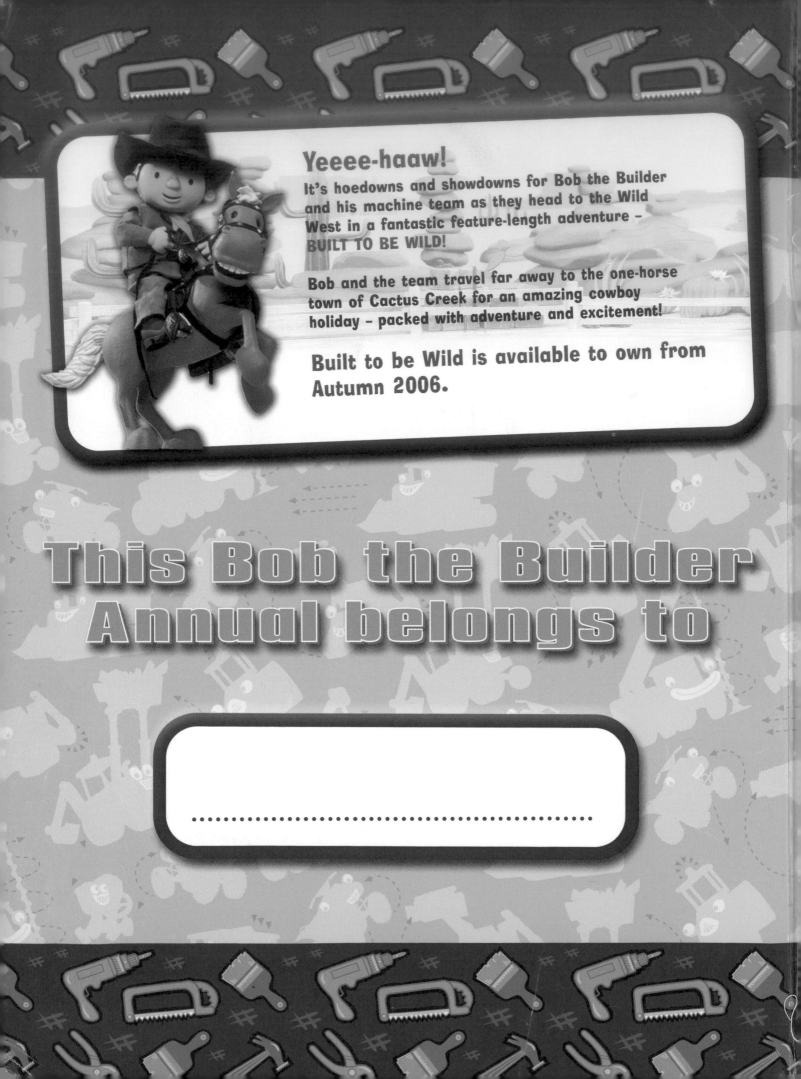

Yeeee-haaw!

It's hoedowns and showdowns for Bob the Builder and his machine team as they head to the Wild West in a fantastic feature-length adventure – BUILT TO BE WILD!

Bob and the team travel far away to the one-horse town of Cactus Creek for an amazing cowboy holiday – packed with adventure and excitement!

Built to be Wild is available to own from Autumn 2006.

This Bob the Builder Annual belongs to

....

Bob the Builder™

PROJECT: BUILD IT

ANNUAL
2007

Contents

Stories adapted from original scripts by Sarah Ball, Rachel Murrell and Marc Seal.

Based on the television series Bob the Builder © HIT Entertainment Limited and Keith Chapman 2006

With thanks to HOT Animation

Text and illustrations © 2006 HIT Entertainment Limited.

The Bob the Builder name and characters and the Wendy, Spud, Lofty, Roley, Muck, Pilchard, Dizzy, Scoop, Scrambler and Benny characters are trademarks of HIT Entertainment Limited. Registered in the UK. All rights reserved.

EGMONT
We bring stories to life

First published in Great Britain 2006 by Egmont UK Ltd
239 Kensington High Street, London W8 6SA
ISBN 978 1 4052 2615 8
ISBN 1 4052 2615 3
Printed in Italy
1 3 5 7 9 10 8 6 4 2

Bob the Builder ™

PROJECT: BUILD IT

"Can we build it? Yes we can!"

Sunflower Valley

Sunflower Valley is a place Bob loves because he used to go there when he was young. He and his family had fun and adventures in the hills, fields and forests, and on the beach.

When Bob heard about plans to build a town in Sunflower Valley he wanted to make sure the valley wasn't spoiled, so he entered the competition to design the new town – and won first prize!

That was the fun part, but now comes the hard work! Bob has to build a town that works with nature and doesn't spoil it. It's a big job but he and his team are going to do it. As they say:

"Can we build it? Yes we can!"

Bob has three important words to help him:
1. **reduce**   **the effects of building on the land, animals, plants and birds**
2. **reuse**   **as many materials as possible**
3. **recycle**   **all sorts of things!**

Say hello to Bob and the team

Bob is a builder who is good at all sorts of building, fixing and mending jobs. He's a great carpenter, painter and plumber.

Pilchard is Bob's pet cat. Her 'job' is to watch TV, eat, sleep and purr!

Wendy is Bob's partner. She's an expert bricklayer and she makes sure the team has all the tools and materials for the job.

Scoop is a big yellow digger and the leader of Bob's machine team. His job is to dig holes and move dirt around.

Roley is a green steamroller. His job is to smooth and flatten dirt and roads using his big rollers.

Bird is Roley's best friend. She likes sitting on his roof and singing with him.

Dizzy is a bright orange cement mixer. Her job is to use her spinning tub to mix up lots and lots of cement and plaster.

Lofty is a blue mobile crane. He does lots of jobs using his special tools: a magnet, a grabber and a demolition ball.

Muck is a red digger-dumper. He does all the messy, mucky jobs like digging, dumping and moving earth around because he just loves being mucky!

Farmer Pickles looks after a busy farm but he always finds time to help Bob and the team if they need him.

Scruffty is Farmer Pickles' puppy. He **thinks** his job is to chase rabbits and bury bones!

Travis is Farmer Pickles' tractor. He and his trailer can do all sorts of useful jobs.

Spud is a scarecrow. His job is scaring crows out in the fields – but he's always hungry, so he **wishes** it was eating!

Squawk the crow's job is making fun of Spud!

Meet Scrambler

Scrambler is the newest member of Bob's team. He's a bright blue all-terrain four-wheel-drive vehicle. Bob won him as part of the competition to design Sunflower Valley. He's very useful because he takes Bob to and from Bobsville and Sunflower Valley. He belongs to Bob but Wendy rides on him sometimes, too.

"Sunflower Valley rocks!"

Scrambler's also useful because he can travel to all parts of the new site – no matter how bumpy or hilly. He has a trailer to help him carry materials from place to place.

"Scram to the Valley!"

Scrambler is happy, friendly and always keen to work. Life for him is just one big, fun adventure. When he's not hard at work he LOVES racing and taking Bob off-roading. He's happiest when Bob puts on his safety helmet and goggles, jumps into the seat and says, "Let's scram!".

Scrambler's extra-wide tyres help him climb and scramble over the roughest ground. They are so fat and bouncy that he can bounce right up into the air!

"Brrrrm!"

The team loves Scrambler – especially Scruffty – because he's so much fun!

Meet Benny

Benny is another new face in Bob's special Sunflower Valley team. He's the youngest of the machine team but that doesn't mean there isn't a lot of hard work for him to do – no way!

"Wheeeee!"

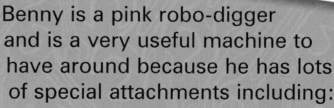

Benny is a pink robo-digger and is a very useful machine to have around because he has lots of special attachments including:
- an industrial grapple
- a side-tip shovel
- an earth drill
- a hammer
- a grader
- a six-in-one shovel

"Speedy Benny"

Benny just loves to work hard and learn new things. He's always eager to help, no matter what Bob asks him to do. He's a whizz at getting the jobs done extra-fast. But that doesn't mean he's careless – he does every job as well as he can.

"Unreal, Banana Peel!"

Benny looks up to Scoop because he's the leader of the team and is bigger and much older than he is. He's given Scoop a special nickname: "Big Banana". Can you guess why?

Benny also gets on very well with Dizzy because, like her, he just loves spinning around as fast as he can!

It's an exciting time for Bob and the team. They're going to build a whole new town in Sunflower Valley! It's time for ...

Bob's fresh start

When the machine team got to Sunflower Valley, everyone looked at the model of the new town Bob had made.

Muck was excited. "People are going to go to school here and live here and work here and play sports here and ..." he said.

"And **we're** going to build it all!" said Scoop.

Just then, Travis the tractor arrived with a new mobile home on his trailer.

"Is that where you're going to live, Bob?" asked Dizzy.

"That's right, Dizzy," said Bob.

Suddenly, the door flew open and Spud the scarecrow looked out. "Are we there yet?" he asked. "I'm starving!"

"What are **you** doing here?" asked Bob.

"I'm Stowaway Spud," said Spud. "I've come to see how you're all getting on."

The mobile home was soon unloaded.

"We have to put it on a hard platform so its wheels don't sink into the ground," Bob told the team. "Let's build it before it gets too dark."

Muck looked worried. "Dark?" he said quietly.

"Yes," said Bob, "it gets very dark out here and we don't have power yet, so we can't turn on the lights or use the oven."

"No oven?" said Spud. "How will we cook food?"

"We'll build a campfire," said Bob. "I need someone to go into the forest to collect firewood. I wonder who?"

Lofty, Roley, Scoop and Dizzy all spoke at once: "**MUCK!**"

Muck looked worried.

"You're not scared, are you?" asked Dizzy.

"Oh, er, course not!" said Muck.

"I know, I'll go with you, Muck," Spud said. "Come on!"

It was dark in the forest and when Muck heard a twig snap, he jumped. "Aaaarrgh!" he cried. "Wait for me, Spud!"

When Spud had collected an armful of branches, Muck looked around. "Shall we go back now?" he asked. Then he heard a **rumble-rumble** noise. "What was that?"

Spud laughed. "My tummy!" he said. "Collecting wood has made me hungry."

Spud was filling Muck's dumper with logs when – **SQUAWK!** – went a bird.

Muck jumped and looked around again. "You do know the way back, don't you?" he asked Spud.

"Course!" said Spud, looking into the trees. "It's through there ... no, it's this way ... no, that ... er ... er ..."

SQUAWK! A bird cried again and this time it was Spud who jumped. "Aaaarrrrggggh!" he said. "What was that? Oh, it's really dark now – and we're lost!"

SQUAWK! The bird cried again.

Louder this time.

"Aaaaarrrrggggh!" cried Muck.

"Aaaaaarraarrrgggghh!" cried Spud.

Muck and Spud ran off into the trees until Muck stopped suddenly. "Look, my tracks!" he said. "We can follow them out of the forest."

* * *

Back at the site, Bob had made a fire.

"I hope Muck and Spud get back soon," he said. "We need more wood."

As he spoke, Muck dashed up and skidded to a halt. "Here's the wood!" he said.

Spud jumped down and sniffed. "Can I smell food?" he asked.

Bob handed him a plate of toast he'd made on the campfire.

"Thanks – **gobble** – Bob – **gobble**," said Spud.

"Where were you two?" asked Scoop. "We were worried."

"Oh, it was – **gobble** – horrid," said Spud between bites of toast. "There were scary – **gobble** – noises and it was dark and – **gobble** – I was worried but – **gobble** – Muck wasn't and then he found the way out!"

"Wow Muck, you're really brave,"

said Dizzy.

"I'm not," said Muck. "I just pretended to be brave so you wouldn't think I was silly."

"Nobody thinks you're silly, Muck," said Bob. "We're all a little bit scared of something."

"I've never been round a campfire before," said Roley.

"And I've never stayed in a mobile home before OR had toast for my dinner!" said Bob.

He laughed and reached for the plate – but all that was left on it were a few crumbs! "Where's all the toast?" he asked.

Munch! Crunch! Munch!
The machines looked around. **"Spuuu-uuu-uddd!"** they said.

Spud wiped his mouth.

"Ooooo, sorry!" he said. "I'll make some more toast, no LOTS more. **Ha-ha**. Spud the toast-maker, that's me!"

Let's talkie-talkie

In Sunflower Valley, Bob and the team often have to work far away from each other. They use their new talkie-talkie machines to keep in touch!

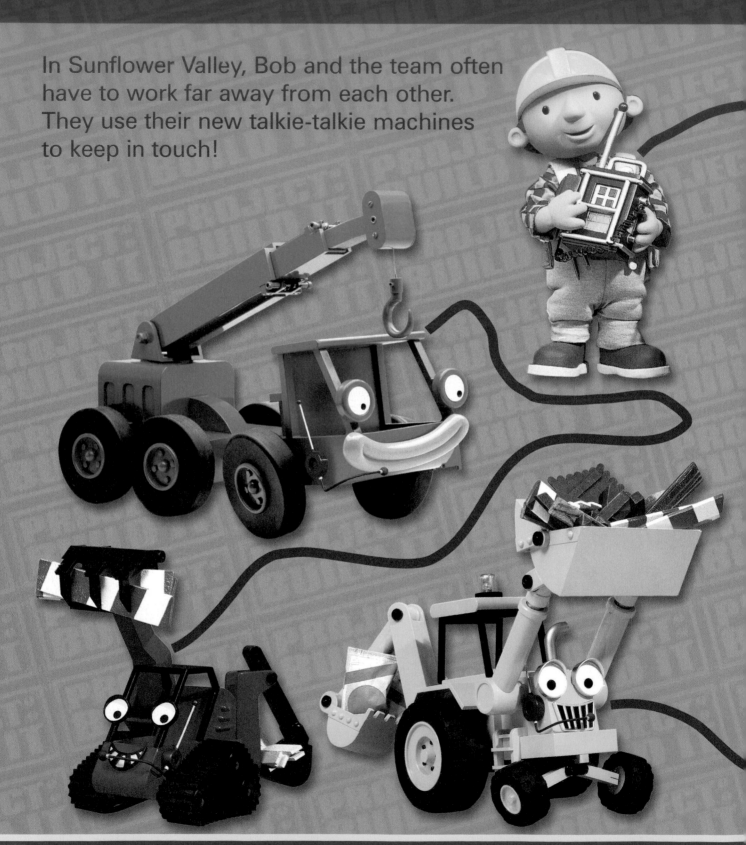

Follow the lines to see who is talking to each other.

ANSWERS: Lofty is talking to Benny, Bob is talking to Scrambler,
Scoop is talking to Dizzy, Wendy is talking to Muck.

When Bob moves to Sunflower Valley, Wendy stays behind to look after the yard until they find ...

Scoop's recruit

1 Wendy was still working at the Bobsville yard. "Let's get thinking, Dizzy," said Scoop. "We need to find someone to take over from Wendy."

2 But first there was a job to do. "Mr Sabatini's got a leak," said Wendy. "Mix up some plaster, Dizzy, and we'll go over to the pizza parlour."

3 Mr Sabatini pointed to a big bulge in his ceiling. "The leak is-a right-a here-a-Wendy," he said, poking it with a brush. "Noooo!" said Wendy.

4 Too late! Water gushed out of the hole and Wendy and Mr Sabatini were soaked. "Mamma mia!" said Mr Sabatini. "Sorry-a-Wendy!"

5

Far away in Sunflower Valley, Bob and the team were busy. "First we need to clear this site so we can build a new yard," Bob told them.

6

Bob got to work getting rid of the thick brambles and bushes. He cut them down then chopped them into small pieces with a shredder.

7

Muck was soon hard at work, too. His job was to shovel up all the big rocks and stones and bits of wood into his big dumper scoop.

8

Then Lofty sorted out all the rocks, branches, stones and weeds that Muck had collected. He made them into separate piles.

9

When the site for the new yard had been cleared, it was Roley's turn. He rolled and rolled the lumpy ground until it was nice and flat.

10

Bob showed Roley how the shredder cut the brambles into small chips. "We'll use them on the paths instead of gravel," said Bob.

11

"We'll use everything here when we start building," Bob explained. "Remember how we're going to work? **Reduce, reuse, recycle!**"

12

Back in Bobsville, Scoop asked the librarian to look for the name of a builder. But she could only find one – Bob. "Ohhh," said Scoop.

13

Scoop told Spud that he was
trying to find a builder for Bob's
yard. "I'm good at building!
Me! Me!" said Spud. "Remember
when I helped Bob's dad?"

14

"Bob's dad!" said Scoop. "Yes,
that's it! He used to be a
builder! Spud, you're a genius!"
Spud smiled. "I am?" he said.
"Er, yeah, I know I am!"

15

Spud rang Robert, Bob's dad,
and asked if he'd help. "Of
course I will," said Robert.
"Come to the yard tonight,"
said Scoop. "But keep it a secret!"

16

In Sunflower Valley, Bob, Muck,
Lofty and Roley looked at the
piles of rock and wood. "This
is great," said Bob. "The new
yard's taking shape already!"

17

"Did you build the old yard?" asked Roley. "No, Dad built it," said Bob. "He built most of Bobsville. That's why they named it after him."

18

Later, Scoop called Muck on the talkie-talkie. "Bring Bob to the old yard," he told him. "But it's a surprise, so don't say why." "I'll get him there!" said Muck.

19

That evening, Muck took Bob back to the old yard where his pet cat, Pilchard, was waiting for him. "It's great to see you, Pilchard," said Bob.

20

Next, Wendy arrived with Dizzy. "Hi, Wendy," said Bob. "Now what's so important that I had to come all the way back from Sunflower Valley?"

21

"I didn't ask you to come back!" said Wendy. Just then Bob heard a loud **COUGH!** from the office. "There's something going on," he said, going inside.

22

"DAD!" said Bob, when he saw his dad sitting at the desk reading a newspaper. "Hello, son," Robert said. "I've come about the job."

23

"But you're retired now, Dad," said Bob. "And what about Mum?" Just then Dot, Bob's mum, appeared. "We're coming back to look after the yard," she said.

24

"Scoop wanted you and Wendy working together again," said Bob's mum. "So here we are." "Good old Scoop," said Bob. "This is the best surprise ever!"

Cool caravan

As soon as Bob's mum and dad came to look after the Bobsville yard, Wendy moved to Sunflower Valley to work with Bob and the team. She has a lovely little caravan to live in. It has a garden full of flowers, a vegetable patch – and a little house for her hens, Henny and Penny!

Look at the two pictures of Bob and his mum visiting Wendy's caravan. The pictures look the same, but there are 5 things that are different in picture 2. Can you spot the differences?

2

ANSWERS: 1. There is an extra light on the path; 2. A flower on the caravan is missing; 3. The door handle is missing; 4. A solar panel on the roof is a different colour; 5. The stripe on the caravan has changed colour.

31

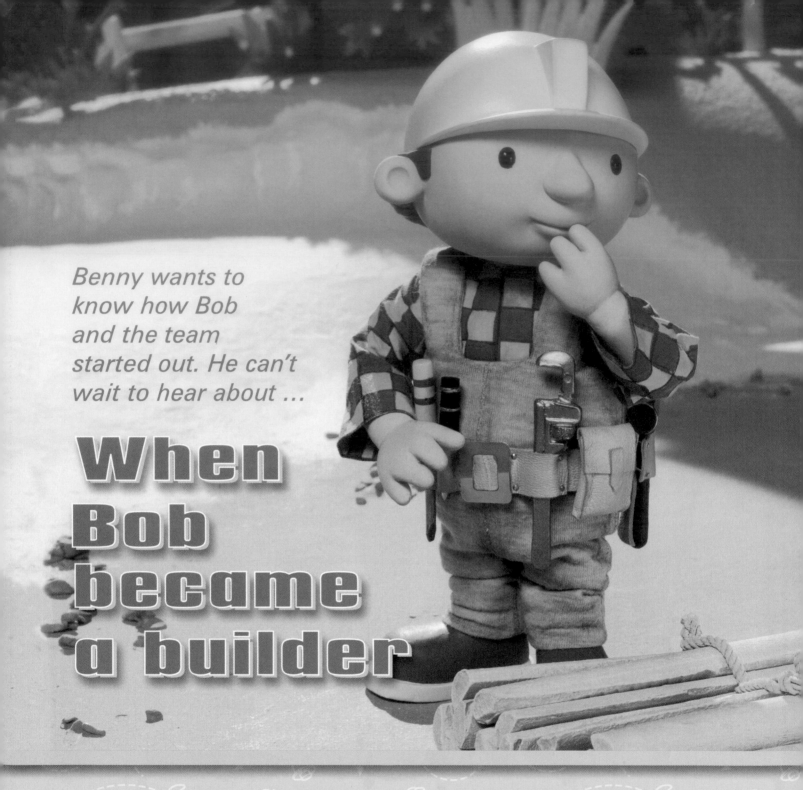

Benny wants to know how Bob and the team started out. He can't wait to hear about ...

When Bob became a builder

Bob and the team were working at the beach. They were going to build a parking area, picnic tables and a playground.

Scoop, Muck and Benny started clearing the ground for the car park.

"This team's unreal!" said Benny. "Who was Bob's first machine, Scoop?"

"ME!" said Scoop. "Bob was working on his own and he needed a machine to help him. He chose me!"

Later on, Benny asked Bob how he had started out as a builder and

Bob told him the story.

"One summer when I was fifteen, I helped Dad build the house and yard in Bobsville," said Bob. "That was when I started to learn about being a builder. First I tried bricklaying. I practised and practised until I got it right, and I never looked back."

"Go on!" said Benny.

"After that I took to building like a hammer to a nail," said Bob. "Dad taught me about carpentry and roofing, tiling and guttering, plastering and painting. Soon we had built a lovely new home and Dad asked me to join the business when I left school. From that day on I wasn't just Bob, I was **Bob the Builder**!"

"What happened next?" asked Benny.

"Things went well and soon I was building whole houses. I had Scoop to help me but we needed more help, so Muck joined the team. He brought his friend Dizzy to help us mix the cement."

* * *

Soon the car park was finished. "Well done, team," said Bob. "Now it's time to help Wendy with the picnic tables."

Benny was hard at work again, but he wanted to know more about Bob's team. "When did you join, Lofty?" he asked.

"When they needed someone who could lift things!" said Lofty.

"And you, Roley?" asked Benny.

"Oh, a little friend called Bird told me Bob needed a roadroller, so I joined the team as well! Bob said, 'Now I have machines that can do everything!'"

"I said, 'I can dig it!'" said Scoop.

"I said, 'I can shift it!'" said Muck.

"I said, 'I can mix it!'" said Dizzy.

"I said, 'I can lift it!'" said Lofty.

"And I said, 'I can roll it!'" said Roley.

"Then Bob won me in the Sunflower Valley competition," said Scrambler.

"And Bob's dad asked me to help!" said Benny. "When did you join the team, Wendy?"

"I've known Bob since we were teenagers but we started working together when Bob needed someone else to help," said Wendy. "I wanted to be a builder – and the rest, as they say, is history!"

The team's next job was to build the playground.

Dizzy, Lofty and Scrambler had collected lots of stuff that had been washed up on the beach. There was an old rowing boat,

a barrel, a bicycle wheel, some drainpipes, driftwood and a fishing net. Bob didn't know what to make with it until – **aaark!** – a seagull picked up a big piece of seaweed and dropped it on his head!

"You look like a pirate with a seaweed beard!" said Scoop.

"**Ha-haaaar**!" said Bob. "Pirate Bob on the seven seas. Hey, I've got an idea! We can use this stuff to build a pirate ship for the children. You know, **reduce** …"

"**Reuse, recycle!**" said the team.

The machines worked hard and soon the pirate ship was finished.

Bob put a pirate flag on the mast and looked through his spyglass.

"Shiver me timbers!" he said.

"All I need now is the captain's crew!"

Just then the team arrived, dressed as pirates!

"Reporting for duty, Captain Bob!" said Wendy.

"Yo-ho-ho! We're the Sunflower Valley pirates!" said Scoop.

Bob smiled. Then he looked at Benny and Scrambler. "How do you like being part of the team?" he asked.

"It's unreal, banana peel!" said Benny.

"Yeah, Bob," said Scrambler. "It rocks!"

"Can we build it?" said Scoop.

"Yes we can!" said the others. All except Lofty. "Er ... yeah ... I think so," he said.

"Ha-ha-harrrrr!" laughed the pirates.

Draw Benny

Draw over the lines to copy the picture of Benny.
It's easy if you do it square by square.

You could colour in both Benny pictures if you like,
then write your name on the line.

Benny by _____

You can help read this story! It's all about ...

Roley's new friend

Listen to the words and when you see a picture, say the name.

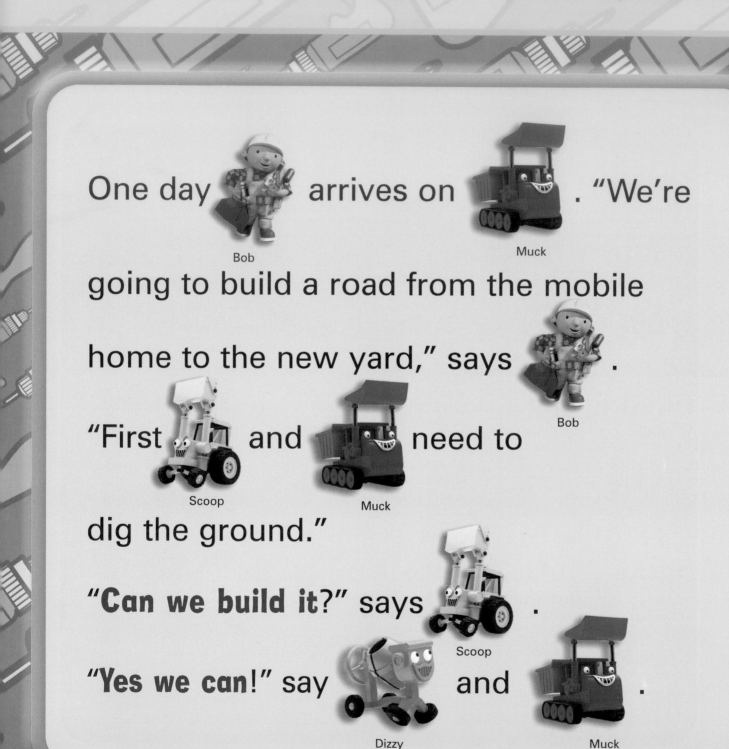

One day arrives on . "We're

Bob   Muck

going to build a road from the mobile

home to the new yard," says .

Bob

"First and need to

Scoop   Muck

dig the ground."

"Can we build it?" says .

Scoop

"Yes we can!" say and .

Dizzy   Muck

"Er, yeah, I think so …" says  .

Lofty

 sees a bird that reminds him of

Roley

his friend  .

Bird

He watches her make a nest. "Don't

build it there,"  tells her. "That's

Roley

where the new road will be."

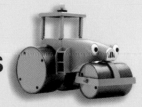

Roley

shows the bird a safe place, but he gets

stuck in the mud! "Help!" says .

Roley

"We need  to roll the new road flat," says Dizzy. "But where is he?"

Scoop has an idea. "Let's ALL roll the road together," he says. "That's a great idea!" says Bob. "Me first!" says Muck.

"Now me!" says Dizzy. "And me!" says Scoop. While they are working, Bob and Lofty go to look for Roley.

"Where are you, Roley?"

42

"Here I am!" 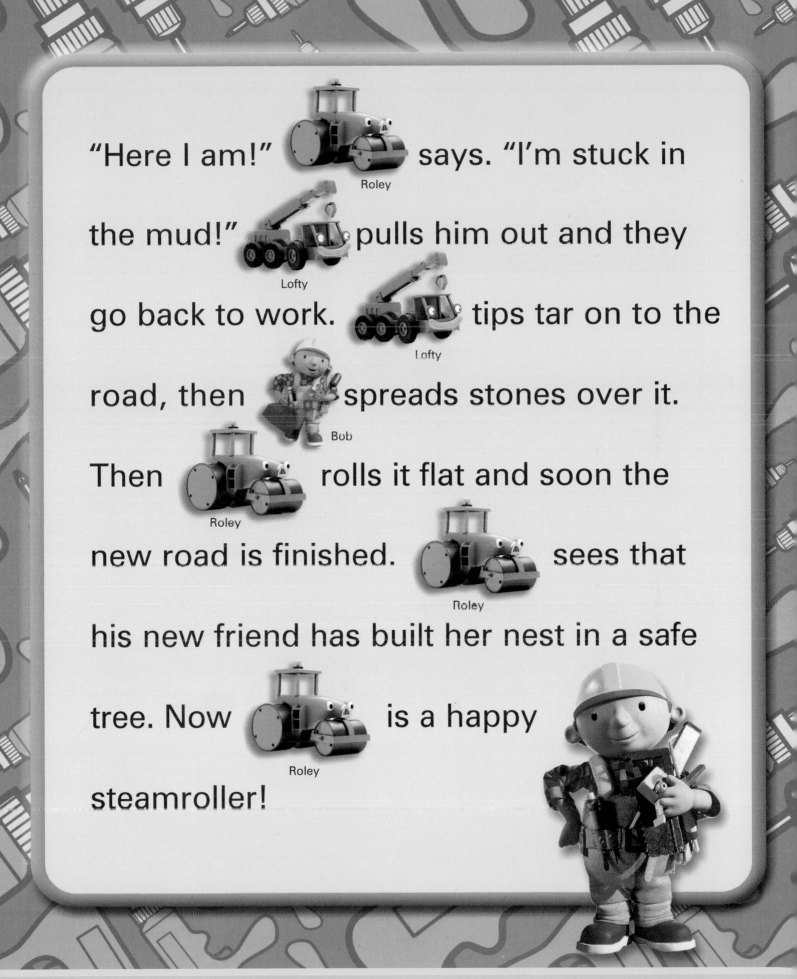 Roley says. "I'm stuck in the mud!" Lofty pulls him out and they go back to work. Lofty tips tar on to the road, then Bob spreads stones over it. Then Roley rolls it flat and soon the new road is finished. Roley sees that his new friend has built her nest in a safe tree. Now Roley is a happy steamroller!

Roley's picture puzzle

Which of these pieces will complete the picture? You can copy and colour them in the spaces if you like.

1

2

3

4

Farmer Pickles is moving to a new farm in Sunflower Valley to grow sunflowers. The new farmhouse is ...

Spud's straw surprise

1

Farmer Pickles, Scruffty and Spud were staying in Bob's mobile home. "Why don't you collect some eggs, Spud?" said Bob, one morning.

2

"Hi, Henny. Hi, Penny," said Spud. "You might be getting new beds, you know! Farmer Pickles brought lots of straw bales yesterday."

3

Later, Spud heard Bob talking about building something made of straw. Spud got the wrong idea. "Oh, no!" he said. "It must be a new scarecrow!"

4

Spud ran away. "I'm going to be left behind in Bobsville," he said. Bob opened the door but all he saw was the basket of eggs. Spud had disappeared!

5

Spud sat on a log and put his head in his hands. "There must be too many birds. Farmer Pickles must need a new SUPER-SIZE scarecrow!"

6

Bob told the team that they were going to build a new farmhouse for Farmer Pickles. "It's a special house," he said. "It's made of STRAW!"

7

"We'll build the walls using straw bales," Bob explained. "Then we'll cover them so the house will be warm and snug and dry," added Wendy.

8

At the yard, Farmer Pickles loaded the straw bales on to Travis' trailer. "Spud will be surprised!" said Farmer Pickles. "I wonder where he is?"

9

Bob's team all had special jobs to do. They were hard at work when Farmer Pickles and Travis arrived with the straw. "**Ruff**!" said Scruffty.

10

Scoop, Benny and Muck dug the foundations then Dizzy mixed lots of concrete and slowly poured it out to make the floor.

11

Bob and Wendy made low stone walls. Then they fixed wooden spikes into them to hold the first row of straw bales in place.

12

Back at the yard, Spud had an idea. "I know," he said. "I'll hide the straw so they won't be able to make a new scarecrow!" And that's what he did!

13

Spud hid the bales in Wendy's caravan, under Bob's mobile home and behind bushes. When Farmer Pickles got back, there were hardly any left.

14

Spud decided to show Farmer Pickles what a good scarecrow he was and he ran around waving his arms in the air. "Shoo!" he cried. "Go away, crows!"

15

"I've never seen Spud work so hard!" said Farmer Pickles. "Ruff!" said Scruffty, running round a tree and bumping into the straw hidden behind it.

16

"Ruff!" said Scruffty, as the bales of straw toppled over. "Now how did they get here?" said Farmer Pickles. "Someone's been hiding 'em!"

17

Spud ran out. "Don't take them!" he said. "You've got me! I hid them so you – **sniff!** – couldn't build a new – **sniff!** – scarecrow. A super-size – **sniff!** – one!"

18

"I don't want a new scarecrow," said Farmer Pickles. "You're a bit of a handful, but you're the best one I've ever had!" Spud smiled. "Oh, thank you!"

19

Farmer Pickles took Spud to see what he had really been making. When it was time for Lofty to make the walls, he sent Spud away.

20

When the walls were done, Bob climbed a ladder and built a wooden frame on top of the bales so the team could fix the roof timbers in place.

21

When the roof was finished, Bob climbed the ladder again and fixed a weather vane to the top to show which way the wind was blowing.

22

At last, the house was finished and Spud was allowed to look. "It's our new farmhouse," said Farmer Pickles. "And you've got your own bedroom!" said Travis.

23

Farmer Pickles had made a little straw scarecrow and nailed it to the door. "It's for our new house, 'Scarecrow Cottage'!" he said.

24

"Wow! Ha-ha-ha! 'Scarecrow Cottage' here I come!" said Spud, opening the door and rushing inside. "Bagsy the top bunk bed! Ha-ha-ha!"

Spud's puzzle

This is a picture of Bob and the team, getting ready to build Farmer Pickles' new straw farmhouse. Spud got a real surprise when he saw it!

Clever Spud has made up a puzzle for you to do.

Which of these little pictures can you see in the big one?
Write ✓ for yes or ✗ for no in each flower.

When Bob asks one of the machine team to look after Scruffty, Scruffty has an exciting race with ...

Off-road Scrambler

After they had built 'Scarecrow Cottage' the next job for Bob and the team was to build a new barn.

"When Farmer Pickles has grown his crop of sunflowers he can store them inside," said Bob.

Scruffty wanted to play.

"**Ruff!**" he said, jumping up at Bob.

"**Ruff! Ruff!**"

Bob had jobs for all the machines except Scrambler.

Scruffty ran around Bob. "**Ruff! Ruff! Ruff!**"

Bob smiled. "Sorry, Scruffty," he said. "I can't play with you right now." Then he turned to Scrambler.

"There **is** a job for you, after all," he told him. "You can look after Scruffty for us."

"Aw, but that's not a proper job," said Scrambler.

"Yes it is," said Bob. "You'll be keeping him safe."

"Yes," said Wendy. "You can take him for a walk."

Scruffty liked the sound of that! **"Ruff!"** he said. **"Ruff! Ruff!"**

"Oh, come on then, Scruffty," said Scrambler.

They went into the woods where Scruffty had fun running around and chasing sticks.

But Scrambler wasn't happy. "Walking a dog!" he said. "I thought I was going to get an important job."

He spoke to Scruffty. "Oh well, if we walk really far maybe you'll

get tired and go to sleep," he said. "Then I can go back and help Bob. Come on!"

"**Ruff!**" said Scruffty.

But Scrambler's plan didn't work. Scruffty ran and ran and it was Scrambler who got tired.

He decided to try a game of hide and seek instead.

"You hide and I'll seek, Scruffty,"

said Scrambler.

"**Ruff!**" said Scruffty as he jumped through a gap in the bushes – and disappeared!

Scrambler chased after Scruffty. "You're supposed to HIDE, not scram!" puffed Scrambler.

But when Scruffty led him down a rough, stony path and leapt over some fallen branches,

Scrambler cheered up. "Hey, you're off-roading, like me!" he said, as Scruffty raced ahead. "Right, want to race, do ya? Here I come! **Wa-haaa!**"

Scruffty and Scrambler raced as fast as they could. Now both of them were having a great time.

When Scruffty jumped off a high hill the sheep watching him were very surprised.

"**Baaaaa!**" they bleated.

"**Baaaaa! Baaaa!**"

Scrambler was right behind Scruffty. "That was great," he panted. "But what about … THIIIIIIS!"

He leapt into the air and landed – **splosh!** – in a muddy pool at the bottom of the hill. He was covered in icky-sticky mud, and so were the sheep.

"**Baa!**" they said angrily. "**Baa!**" When Scrambler had got his

breath back, he drove out of the muddy pool. He was tired out – but very, very happy.

"It's been hard work playing with you," he told Scruffty. "But good fun!"

Scruffty yawned and leaned against Scrambler. They BOTH looked sleepy now …

Back at the site, the team had been working really hard. The barn was finished and Bob and Wendy were having a cup of tea when Farmer Pickles, Travis and Scrambler arrived.

"Where's Scruffty?" asked Wendy.

"He's right here," whispered Farmer Pickles, lifting up a blanket on Scrambler's seat.

There was Scruffty, fast asleep!

"They were **both** asleep when

we found them!" said Travis.

"I wasn't sleeping," said Scrambler. "I was just … er … resting!" Then he noticed the barn. "Wow! You've finished it!"

The noise woke Scruffty, who jumped down and gave Scrambler a big lick.

"Hey, get off, that tickles!" laughed Scrambler.

"I think Scruffty likes you,

Scrambler," said Farmer Pickles.

"Well, he's a really great dog!" said Scrambler. "And we're off-roading buddies now!"

"You did three important things today," said Bob. "You kept Scruffty out of the way, made sure he was safe … and you made a new friend!"

"Wicked!" said Scrambler.

"**Ruff!**" said Scruffty. "**Ruff! Ruff! Ruff!**"

Colour in Scrambler

Scrambler looks really smart – when he's clean! But he loves off-roading so he's often covered in mud!

Colour in this picture of Scrambler using the spot-colour code as neatly as you can. Complete your picture by drawing lots of sacks and pipes to fill his trailer, then write your name on the line.

scrambler by _____

When Muck sees Marjorie's flat-pack house and Farmer Pickles' straw farmhouse, he decides he wants to build his own special house. He calls it ...

Muck's mud hut

1

Bob showed the team their next job. "It's a flat-pack house, a sort of kit house," he told them. "It's for Marjorie who's going to work in the sunflower factory."

2

Benny and Muck were out exploring when they met Marjorie. She was staying in a little blue-and-yellow tent until her flat-pack house was ready.

3

When they met Spud he told them how much he liked his straw house. "I love it!" he said. "It's a house built of my very favourite thing, straw!"

4

"I'd like a house made of my favourite thing," said Muck. "Mud!" Benny laughed. "And I'd like one made of snow," he said. "I love snow!"

5

Back at the site, Scoop dug the foundations for the house and Bob told Muck and Benny to take the soil to the yard. "Take your talkie-talkies!" he said.

6

When they met Spud, Muck showed him the muddy soil. "You could build a mud hut with that!" said Spud. Muck gasped. "You're a genius!" he said.

7

"We'll build my mud hut near the river," said Muck. "It's the perfect place because we can get water and more mud if we need it," he said.

8

Muck used old posts from the recycling pile at the yard to build the frame for his hut. "You know what Bob says, '**reduce**, **reuse**, **recycle**'!" he said.

9

Soon the hut had a straw roof. "Unreal, banana peel!" said Benny. "Now we need mud – loads of it!" said Muck. Spud liked the sound of that!

10

Back at the house site, the walls were up. Bob was showing Marjorie how to fix the solar panels to the roof, while Wendy worked on the decking.

11

Things weren't going very well down by the river. Muck, Benny and Spud had stopped putting mud on the hut and were throwing it at each other instead!

12

Muck got more mud from the river bank. But he took too much and the bank burst! Water rushed out and washed away Muck's mud hut.

13

"Look, the water's heading for Marjorie's tent!" said Benny. "Oh, no," said Muck. "This wasn't supposed to happen. I can't look!"

14

The water rushed through the field and took Marjorie's tent with it. Muck spoke into his talkie-talkie: "Emergency! We need help, over."

15

Bob heard Muck's voice on Scoop's talkie-talkie. "It's the river! It's burst its banks," said Muck. "Action stations, team," said Bob. "Let's go!"

16

Muck was bravely using his digger to hold back the water when Scoop and the team arrived. Bob hammered wood into place to seal the gap.

17

Then Bob and Spud used sandbags to build up the bank. "Right, Muck, move away now," said Bob. "Gently does it." Hooray! The bank held!

18

Muck had some explaining to do. "We used mud from the river bank to build a mud hut," he said. "But water whooshed out and washed it away!"

19

Lofty arrived with Marjorie's tent on his hook. "Where is Marjorie going to sleep now?" said Benny. "In her new house," said Bob. "I'll show you!"

20

Over at the house site, Bob fixed the last solar tiles to the roof and Marjorie rolled a big green water tank into place to collect rainwater.

21

"That's the outside done," said Bob. "We'll start on the inside tomorrow." Marjorie smiled. "I can't wait for my family to see the new house," she said.

22

"We're really sorry about your tent," said Muck. "Don't worry, the inside of the house isn't finished but I can still sleep in there," said Marjorie.

23

Muck and Benny were still covered in mud. "It's time to clean you two up now!" said Bob. "Yeah, I've had enough muck for one day," said Muck.

24

Bob laughed. "I never thought I'd hear you say that, Mucky Muck!" he said. Muck giggled. "Neither did I!" he said. "Mucky Muck's had enough! **Ha-ha**!"

Bob's quiz

Bob has made up a tricky quiz for you. Can you answer all ten questions? Look back through the book to find the answers.

1 Who gave Scoop his new name, "Big Banana"?

2 In the story "Scoop's recruit", who poked a hole in the ceiling?

3 Whose pet puppy is Scruffty?

4 Who is this? She stayed in a tent until her new house was built.

5 What are the names of Bob's mum and dad?

6 In the story "When Bob became a builder", who was Bob's first machine?

7 What did the team use to build "Scarecrow Cottage"?

8 In the story "Off-road Scrambler", which farm animals did Scrambler splash with mud?

9 What is the name of Farmer Pickles' tractor?

10 Wendy has two hens. Are their names:
a. Lenny and Benny
b. Henny and Penny or
c. Cluck and Chuck?

Check your answers at the bottom of the page.
Did you answer all the questions?
Well done! Now draw your face in the space and write your name.